# A Wave Came Through Our Window

Zetta Elliott

# A Wave Came Through Our Window

Illustrated by Charity Russell

Rosetta Press

# Books by Zetta Elliott

A Wish After Midnight

An Angel for Mariqua

Bird

Dayshaun's Gift

Fox & Crow: a Christmas Tale

I Love Snow!

Max Loves Muñecas!

Room In My Heart

Ship of Souls

The Boy in the Bubble

The Deep

The Girl Who Swallowed the Sun

The Last Bunny in Brooklyn

The Magic Mirror

The Phoenix on Barkley Street

Last night a wave came through our window.

Not a splashing, salty wave.

Not a greedy, hungry wave that tugs at your ankles as you run up the beach.

It was a different kind of wave.

In the summer, we sleep with the windows open WIDE.

It gets real hot in our apartment, so Benny and I sleep in our underwear.

Papa tells us to lie still, but hot nights make you feel itchy inside.

Benny and I toss and turn.

We kick off the sheets and slide our hands under our pillows 'cause that's where the cool is at.

The air in our bedroom feels warm and thick like
Grandma's split pea soup. The fan on our dresser turns
and churns the air, but doesn't cool the room at all.
Benny and I hold our hands up high and wait for the first
wave to come through our window.
Sometimes it comes right away.
Sometimes we have to wait.
I spread my fingers wide apart and look out at the moon.
It is bright and round like a big white zero in the middle
of the dark blue sky.
Benny's arms aren't as strong as mine.
She gets tired of waiting and starts to whine.
"When's the wave going to come?"
"Shhh," I tell her. "It's coming now. I can feel it."
Sounds and smells pour through the window,
filling the shadowy corners of our room.

Benny and I float in the darkness, our beds like islands
in the sea of night.
The wave washes over us, stirring the air and sharing
secrets from our neighbors' homes.
"I smell incense," says Benny. "That must be Meroë."
Meroë lives right above us. She burns smoky incense
and lights candles at night.
The air in our room smells spicy and sweet,
like sandalwood and vanilla.
Benny and I lie still and listen for Meroë's special bell.
After it rings, we can hear Meroë chanting softly while
she meditates.

Then a new wave comes through the window, bringing
fresh smells and sounds.
Cool blue notes slide out of a saxophone and seep
through the screen.
Mr. Berkowitz is out on his fire escape, listening to jazz
music while he smokes a cigar.
Benny says, "Oh, yeah," and snaps her fingers
to keep time.
The music makes me want to scat:
"Beboppalubadoodubaweewallabibbitybeepadingdonghey!"
I think I sound just like Ella Fitzgerald,
but Benny still cracks up.

The night air swirls around us before draining out the
window once more. But like the tide, within seconds it
comes rushing back in.
I take a deep breath and then quickly plug my nose.
"Yuck!" Benny puts her pillow over her face.
Mrs. Pinkett in the building behind us is
frying up some fish.
Escovitch fish tastes delicious, but it sure smells kind of
funky right now!
The cats in the back alley howl with hunger.
Benny takes her pillow off her face and joins in.
We both screech like alley cats until Mama hollers at us
to cut it out.

Benny and I are glad when the fish smell goes away. The next wave that comes through our window brings air that is rippling with rhythm.

Ana and Felix Lopez live below us. They're newlyweds. We can't understand the Spanish words they're singing, but we know all that laughter means they're having fun.

"Mira, mira!" cries Benny. She jumps up on her bed and tries to dance the merengue.

I laugh so hard my ribs start to ache.

Papa sticks his head in our room, and Benny bounces back into bed.

"You two should be asleep by now," Papa says with warning eyes.

Benny and I giggle and close our eyes while we wait for the next wave to come in.

For a little while there is just silence.

Benny starts breathing heavily and I can tell

she is falling asleep.

And then, just as my eyes are about to close, the softest

wave slips into our room.

Benny rolls over and looks at me.

"What's that?" she asks in a whisper.

I get out of bed and go over to the window.

There is a man sitting on the fire escape of the building

behind ours. He is holding something up to his lips.

Benny crawls out of bed and stands beside me.

"Is he kissing it?"

I nudge Benny to make sure she's awake.

"That's just how you play it," I tell her.


The man's slender brown fingers dance along the flute.

Whispery notes rise up into the night sky and then drift

down into the alley like snow.

Benny and I shiver and go back to bed.
It's still hot in our bedroom, but we are
ready to sleep now.
Benny starts snoring almost right away.
I hear my parents' laughter coming from the living room.
A plane rumbles in the sky as it flies overhead.
The moon still looks like a big white zero in the middle
of the dark blue sky.
I yawn and close my eyes.

## THE END

# ABOUT THE AUTHOR

Born in Canada, Zetta Elliott moved to the US in 1994. Her books for young readers include the award-winning picture book *Bird*, *A Wish After Midnight*, *Ship of Souls*, and *The Deep*. She lives in Brooklyn and likes birds, glitter, and other magical things.

Learn more at www.zettaelliott.com.

# ABOUT THE ILLUSTRATOR

Charity Russell has always loved drawing and has had a strange attraction to books, especially square ones! Becoming a children's book illustrator therefore seemed the perfect job for her, so she did a degree and then a Masters degree in Illustration and Design. She was born in Zambia to an Irish mum and English dad, and moved around a bit until settling in England as a teen. She can easily get lost in her work and likes creating strange worlds, objects, and creatures (her children included).

Learn more at www.charityrussell.com

CPSIA information can be obtained at www.ICGtesting.com
Printed in the USA
LVIW01n2140050317
526223LV00007B/16